The Strange School

Canada

Hilts, Katherine M., 1983- , author
    The Strange School/ Katherine Hilts ; illustrated by Gabe Kong

ISBN: 9781778005305

Visit: www.kathilts.com

The Strange School

Written by Katherine Hilts

Illustrated by Gabe Kong

~ For my current and former students;

thank you for continually teaching and inspiring me

In a strange, strange city

On a strange, strange street

There's a strange, strange school

That you would NOT want to meet

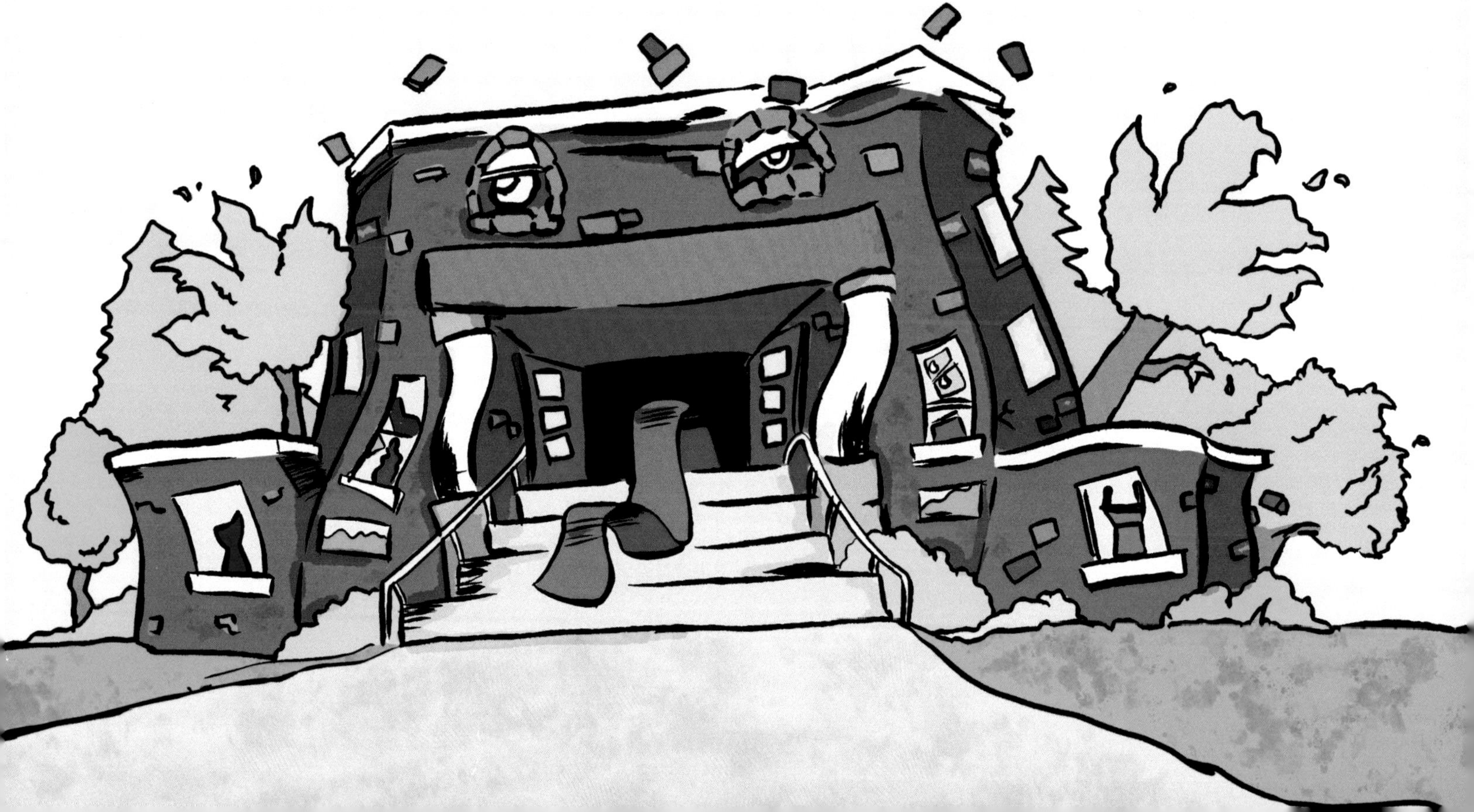

When I first walked through the doors

it seemed like any other school

As I look back now of course,

I understand that I was a fool

The fountains, for starters, spray at will

and some days just won't stop!

The hallways turn to rivers

and your homework to mushy slop!

On those slippery days, grab your canoe

(made of wood or fiberglass)

Leave your work to float away,

and row your way to class

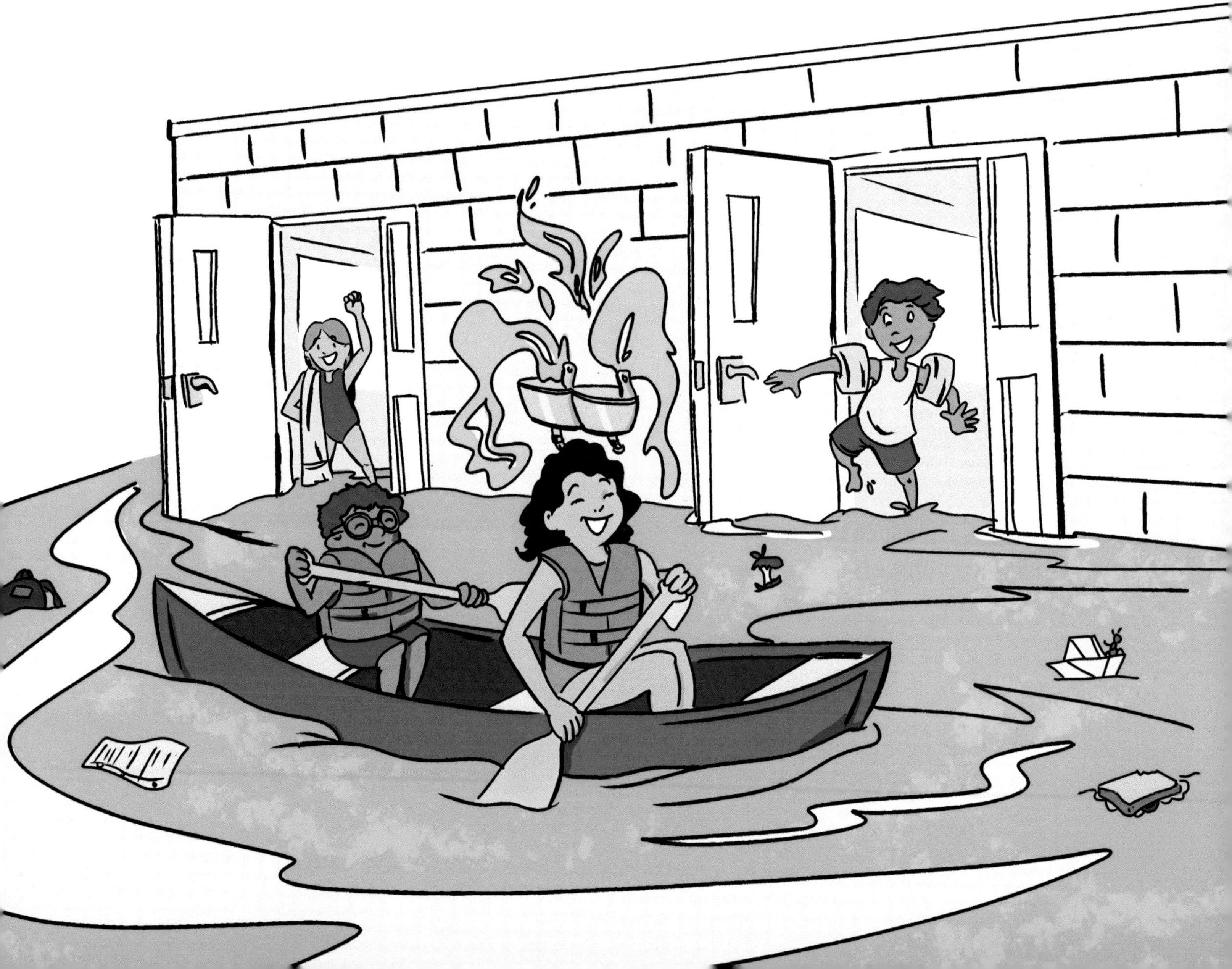

It's not unusual to get distracted
during lessons, that's true
But the classrooms in this strange school
leave everything askew!

The pencils find it amusing
to bounce around on their erasers
My first classroom job was a
'Pencil with Eraser Chaser'

They'll jump on desks, legs, heads,
and soar through the air
Sometimes landing on the teacher's nose
and giving them a scare

I would suggest bringing a net,
as they CAN be pointy and mean
Also, bringing something with extra bounce,
like a mini-trampoline

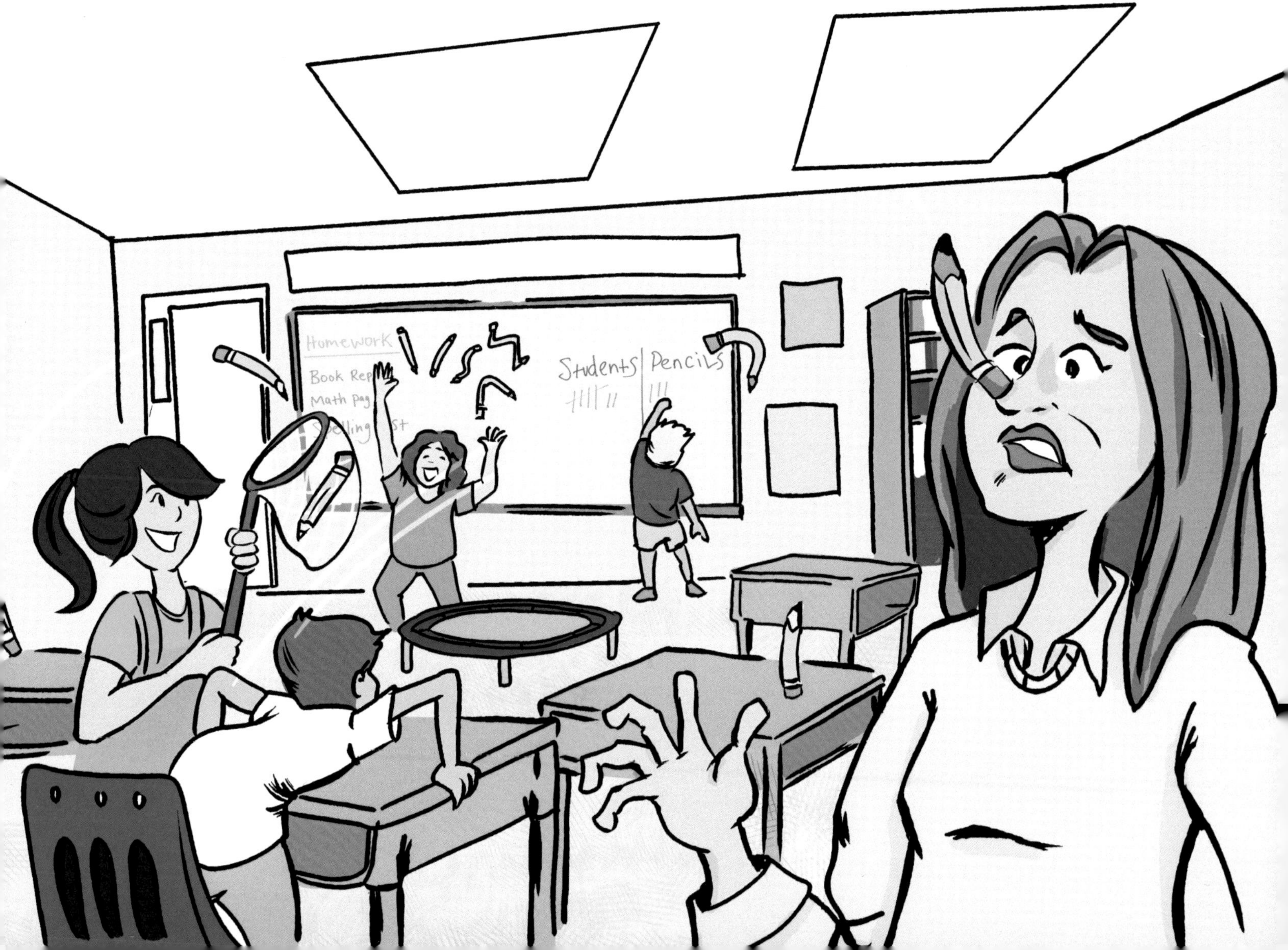
Homework
Students
Pencils

You'll catch so many that your teacher will smile

and say, 'Wow! You're so smart!'

But I'm sorry to inform you

that the pencils are just the start...

The books are really, quite rude

and often burp or fart

And during story time

ALWAYS skip to their favourite part

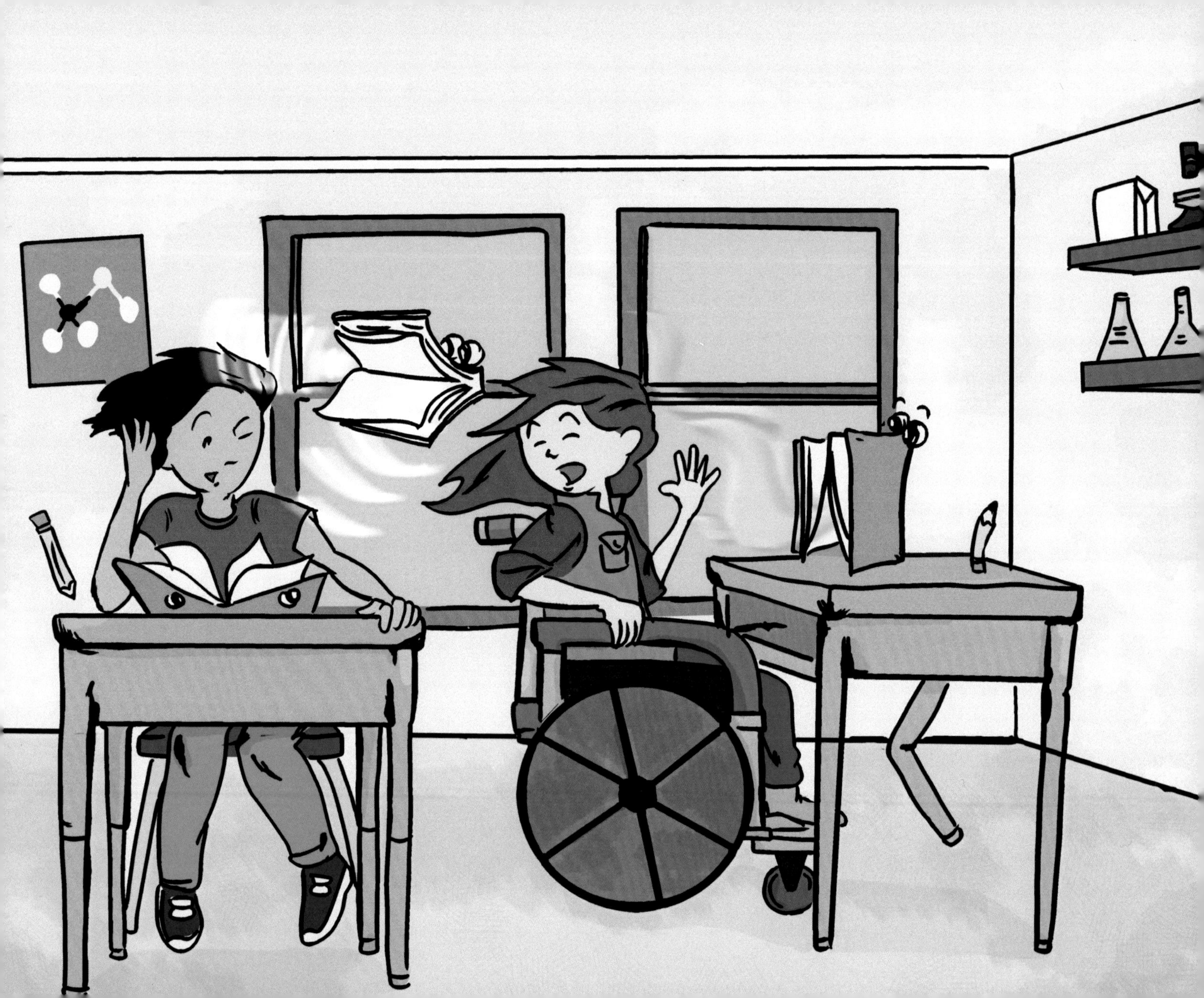

The desks and chairs move around

so they're always out of place

But it IS fun starting the day

with a friendly game of chase!

I *would* however recommend

that you bring some chewing gum

Did I mention that the desks have teeth?

Much better they chew the gum

Than your finger or your thumb!

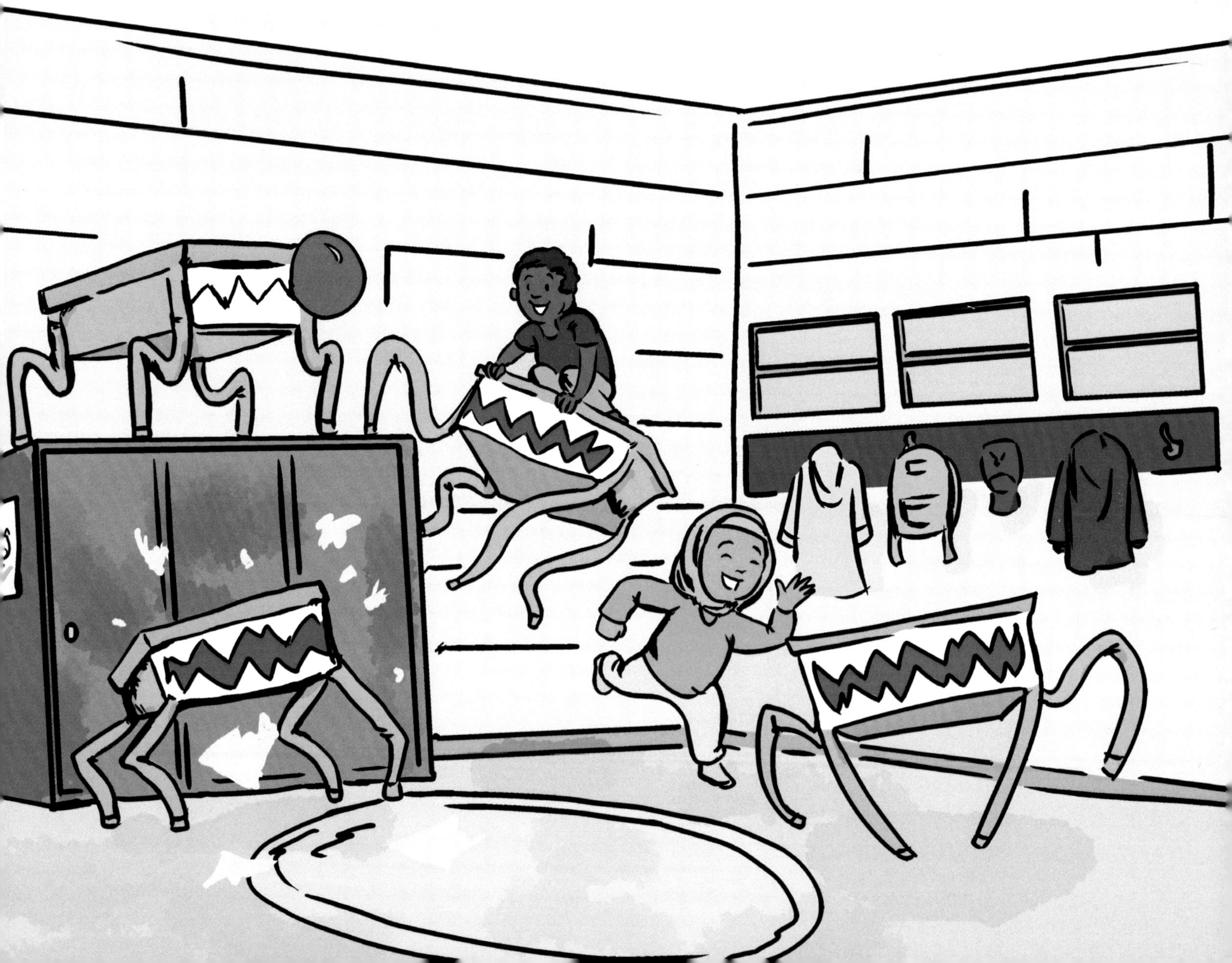

I suppose even desks get cranky

maybe they need more rest?

Perhaps gluing them in place could help,

Yes- I think that would be best.

It's also helpful to sing whenever

your desk is being a pest

They tend to get extra jumpy

right before a test

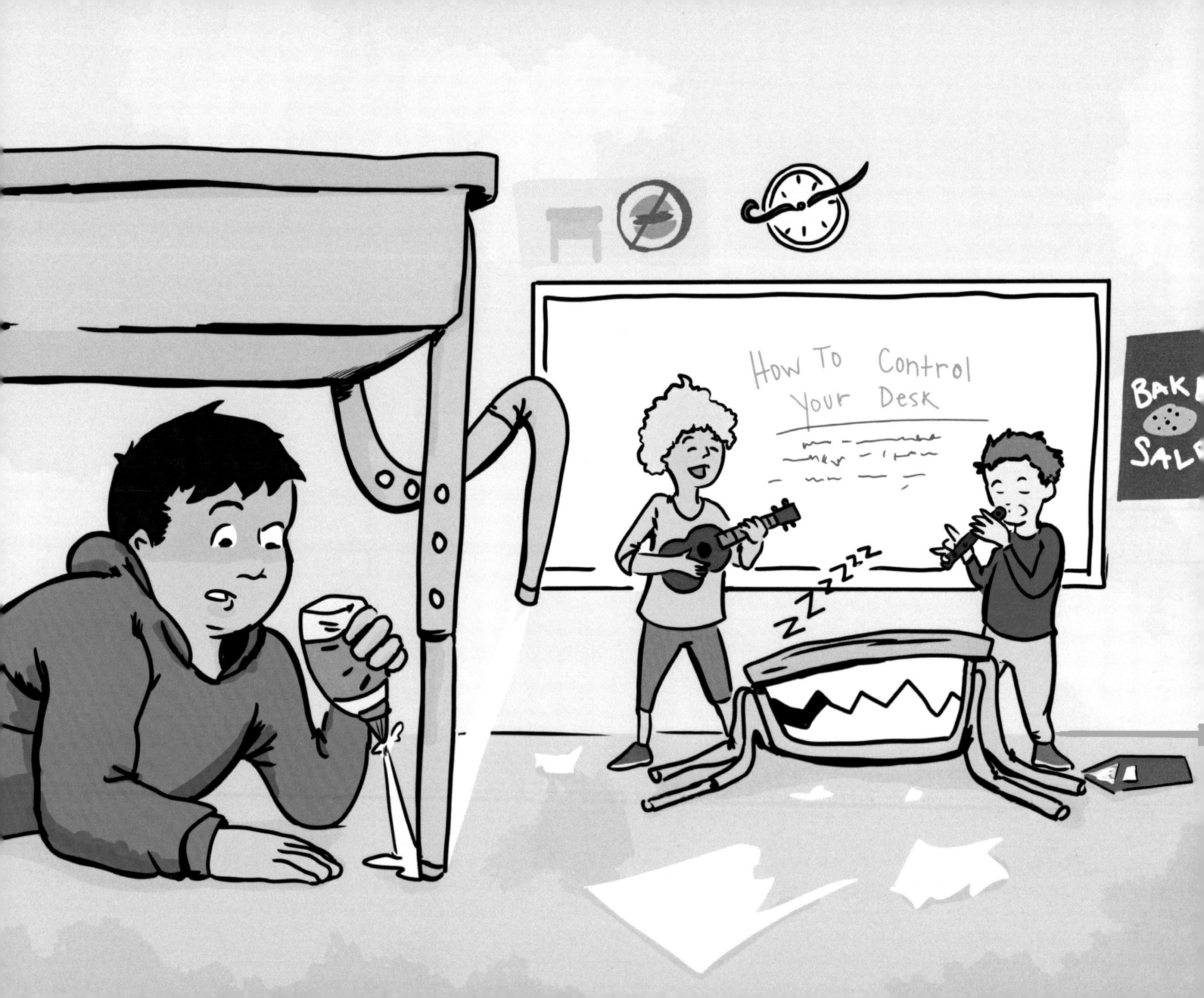
How To Control Your Desk
ZZZZZZZ

When it's time for Art, be warned!
You'll need to be on your toes!
The paint brushes don't like to stop painting
and will decorate your clothes

The scissors get carried away
and zig-zag here and there
Some dream of working in salons
and prefer to cut your hair

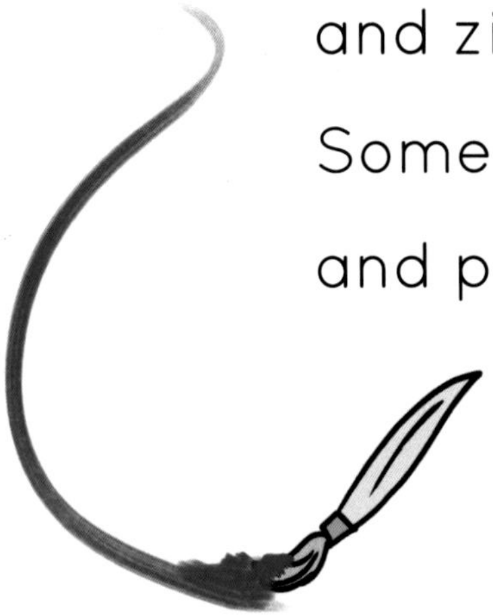

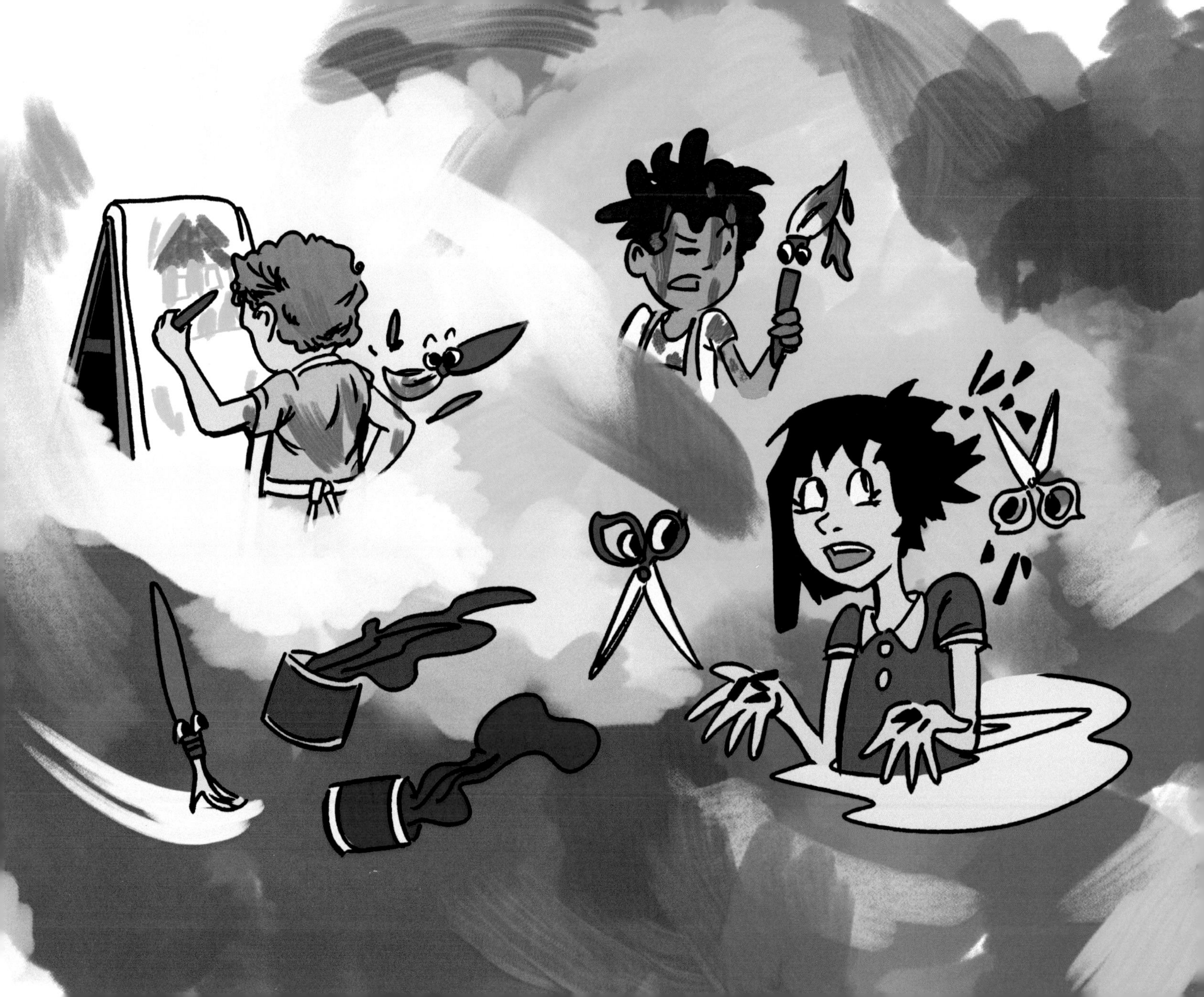

I should warn you about the gym

to be more precise, the storage room bin

You see, many creatures live in there,

so the balls are afraid to go in!

When your teacher says 'Cleanup!'

that's when your troubles begin

The balls bounce away and attempt to hide...

Under shirts, on heads, they twist, flop and spin!

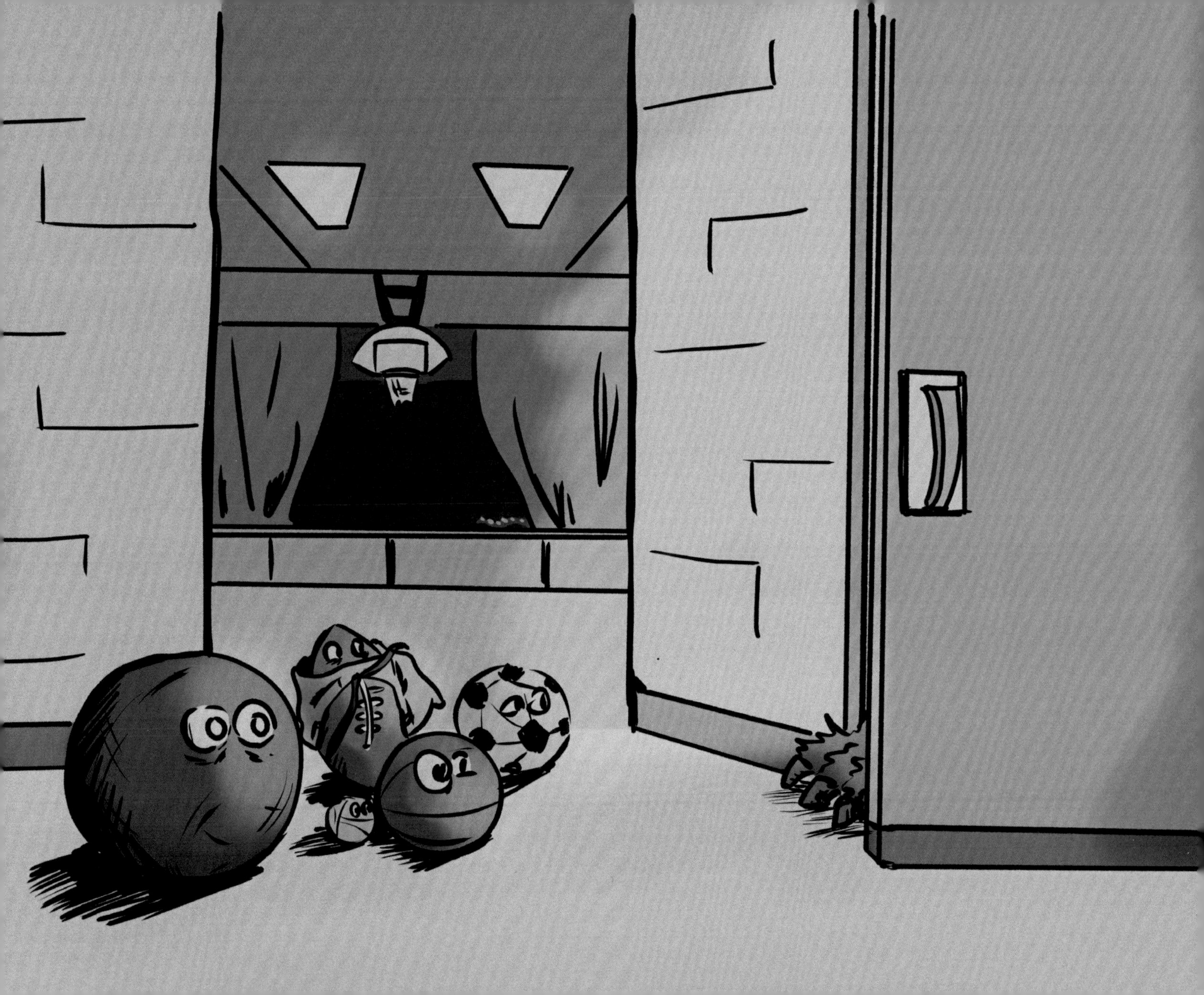

By this point you must be wondering

what sort of principal

could allow such SILLINESS!

Are they a comedian? A CLOWN?

I do have my suspicions on the matter- but please

Make sure you're sitting down.

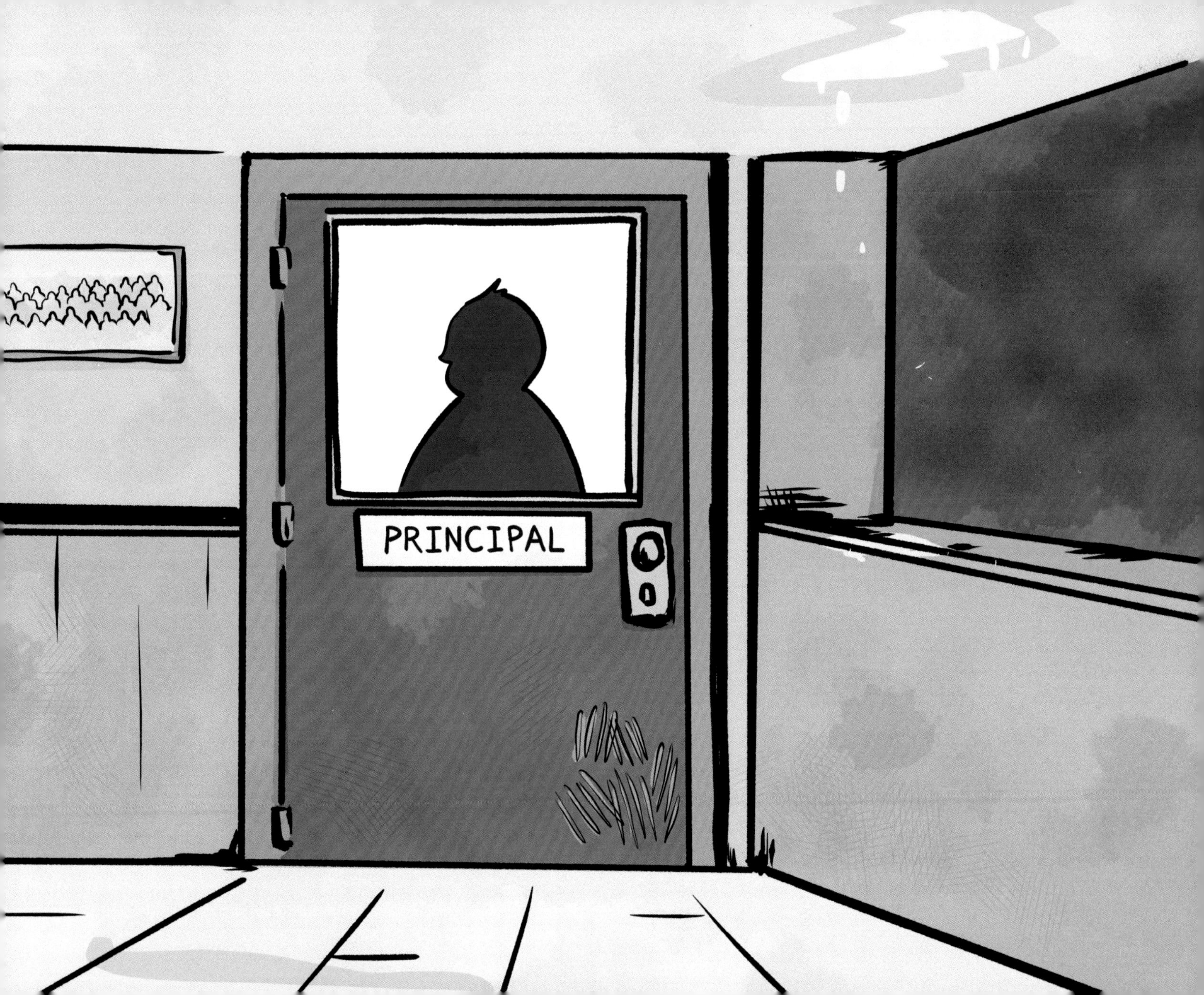
PRINCIPAL

One day, I had to stay late after school

(because my scissors had cut off my eyebrow)

And what I saw in the office was SO shocking,

I haven't told anyone until now

The principal's door was slightly ajar

and the air smelled of tuna somehow

I turned my head to listen

and heard a harrowing *'MEOW!'*

A human disguise fell to the floor with a *splat.*

Revealing that the principal is *actually* a...

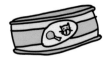

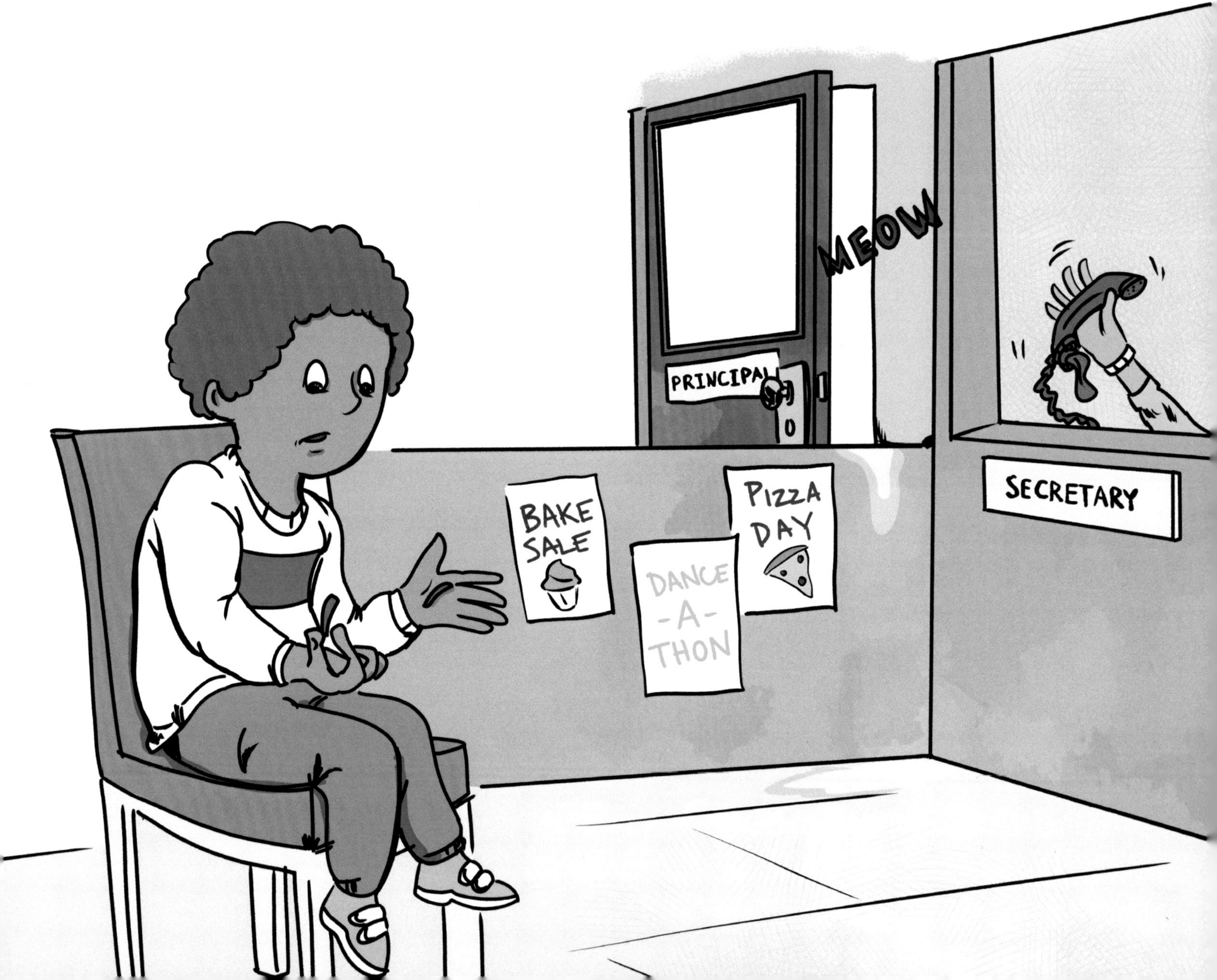
MEOW
PRINCIPAL
SECRETARY
BAKE SALE
DANCE -A- THON
PIZZA DAY

CAT!

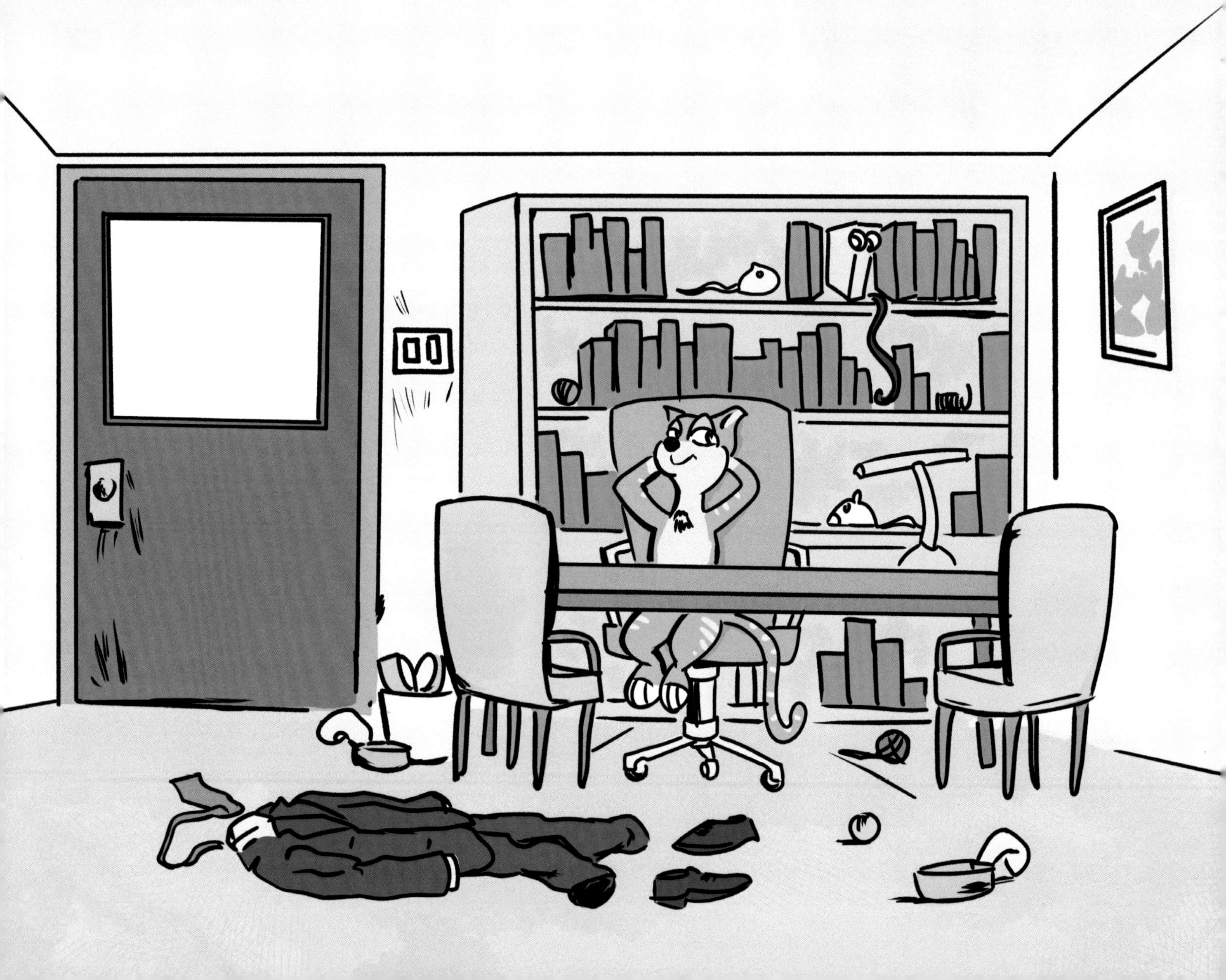

Suddenly it all made sense!
This SILLY school is being run by a CAT!
That's why there are 'NO DOGS ALLOWED'
posters everywhere
That's why you'll not see a bird, mouse or rat!

When I think about it, I'm grateful
and don't want to leave too soon
After all, it could be worse,
My cousin's school is being run by a...

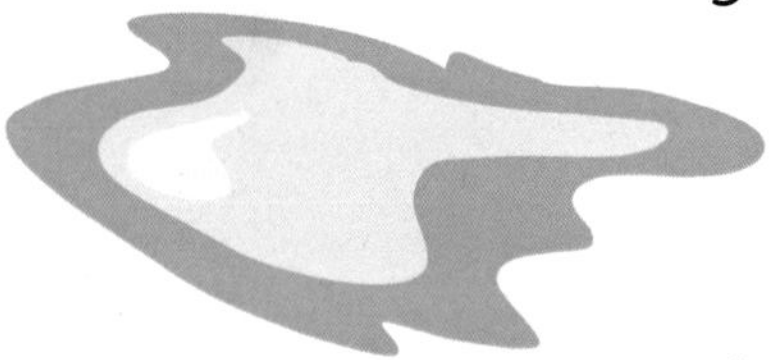

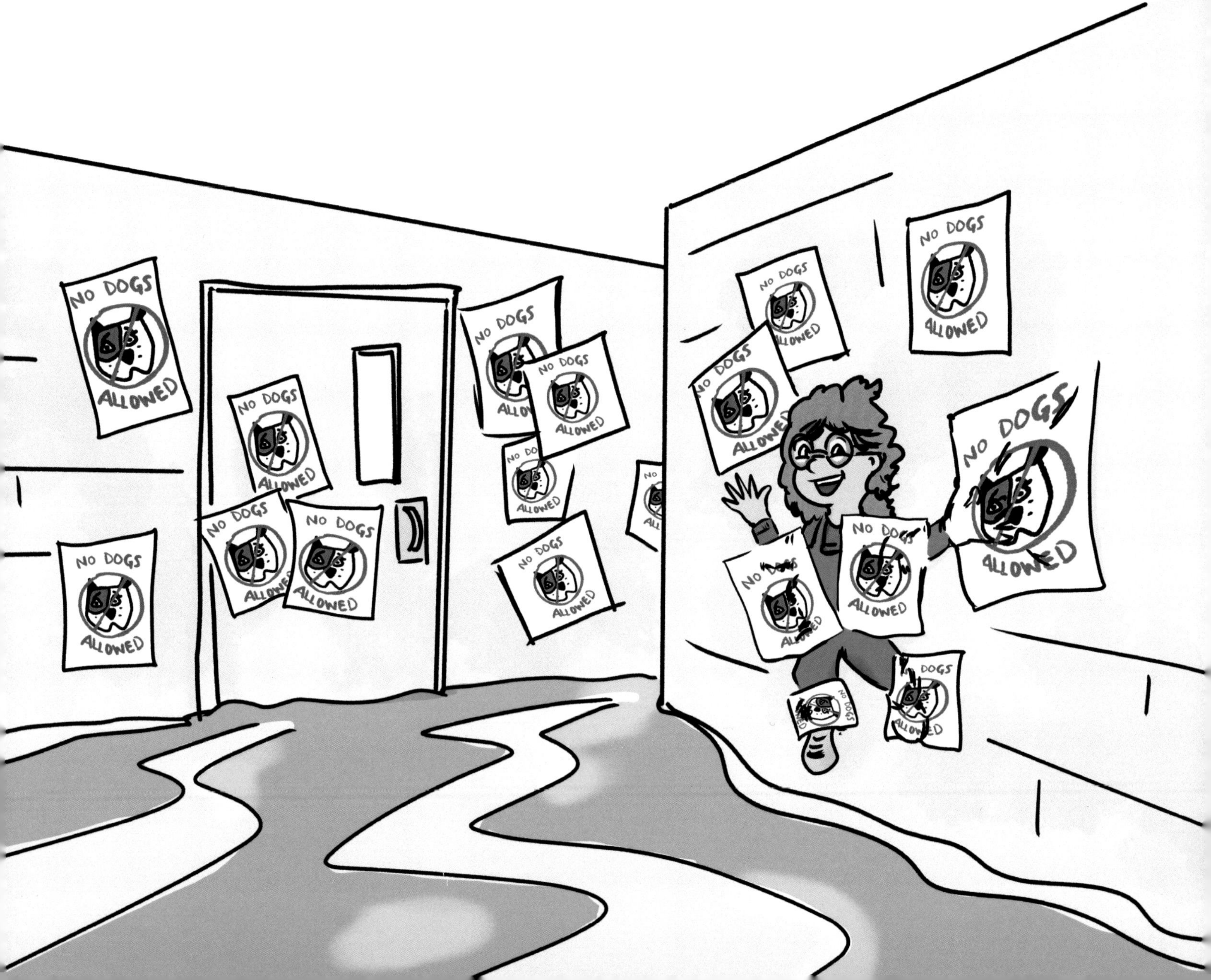
NO DOGS ALLOWED

RACCOON!

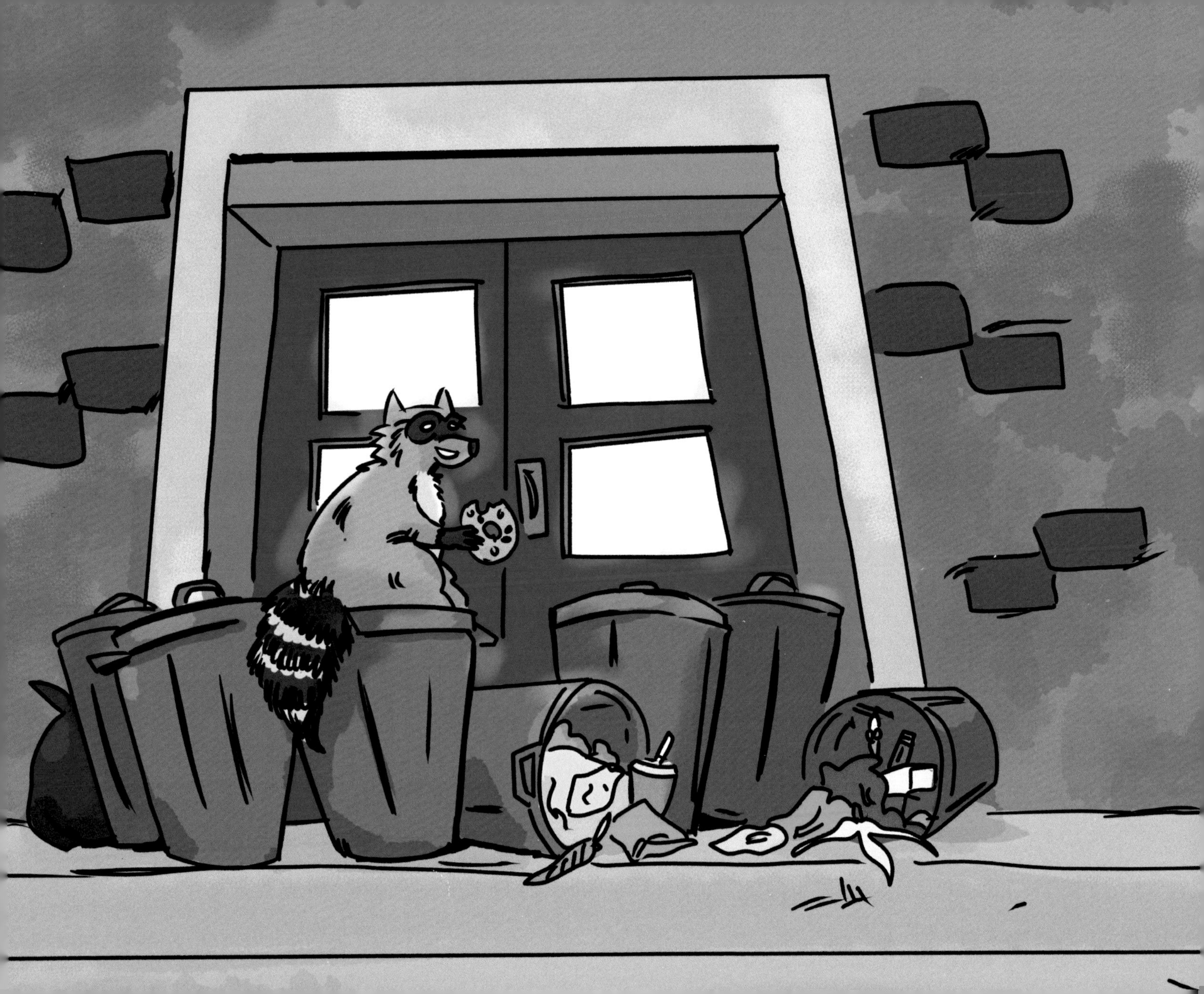

School Supply List:

- ☐ Canoe (to get to Class)
- ☐ Bathing Suit and Towel
- ☐ Chewing Gum (for hungry desks)
- ☐ Bug Net
- ☐ Mini Trampoline
- ☐ Ukulele (for singing to desks)
- ☐ Hard Hat
  (to protect your head and
  Prevent hair from being Cut)
- ☐ Cans of Tuna
  (to bribe the Principal)